AMY SCHWARTZ

Begin at the Beginning

A Little Artist Learns about Life

KATHERINE TEGEN BOOKS
An Imprint of HarperCollins*Publishers*

When Sara got home from school, her mother was in the kitchen, baking cookies.

"How was school today, dear?" she asked.

"Today," Sara told her mother, "was horrible. First my clay pot collapsed.

"Then my toothpick tree fell apart.

"And then Ms. Weinstein picked me to do the class painting for the art show tomorrow. She said she knew I could do something *wonderful*."

"But that *is* wonderful," her mother said.

"No it's not. I don't have even one idea!" Sara said. "I was going to paint the tree outside my window—but that's too easy. I have to think of something very important. I'll get started immediately after this butter-and-jelly sandwich."

Sara made herself two butter-and-jelly sandwiches and ate them one after the other. Then she ate three chocolate-covered graham crackers and a pretzel.

"Now," Sara said, "I am ready to begin."
First Sara cleared off her desk.

Then she set out her box of twenty-four Very Fine Watercolors and filled her jelly glass with water.

She unpacked the fat, round brush and the pad of bright white watercolor paper her grandmother had given her last year.

Then she sat down to work.

"Now," Sara said, "I am going to paint the most wonderful painting that has ever been painted."

Sara thought for a moment.

"I know: I will paint the earth—and the sky—and the day and the night, and-the-summer-and-the-winter-and-everything! I will paint the universe! Everyone will be amazed!"

Sara looked at her blank paper.
"But I wonder where the earth should go," she thought.

"Maybe it should go here.

"No. Maybe it should go there.

"Maybe I need another sandwich."

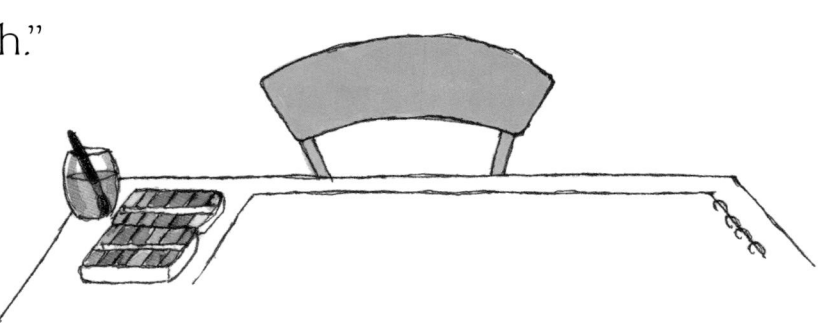

Twenty minutes later, Sara tried to start again.

"All right," she told herself. "Now, I am going to begin."

She picked up her brush and painted a long blue line. It didn't look right at all. She crumpled up the paper and threw it on the floor.

Sara started one painting after another.

"These paintings are not wonderful at all," Sara moaned. "Painting the whole world is harder than I thought."

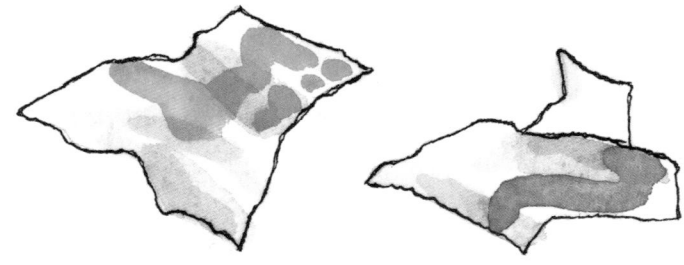

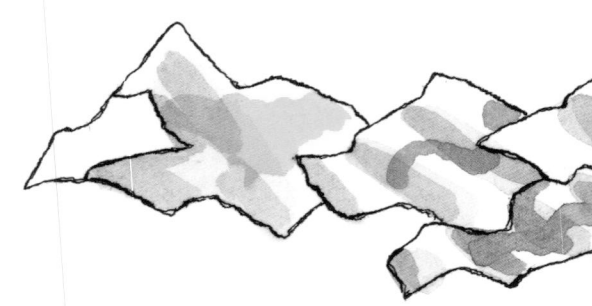

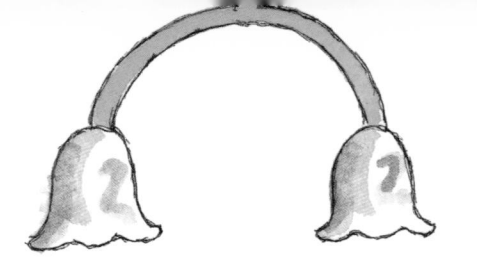

"Maybe this paper is too small," she thought.
"Or maybe this brush is too large.
"Maybe twenty-four watercolors are not enough!
"Maybe," thought Sara, "I should change my rinse water."

And she took her jelly glass into the bathroom.

Sara emptied the water into the sink. She frowned
into the mirror and saw Ms. Weinstein frowning back.

"I am expecting a
wonderful painting, Sara!

"Everyone is depending on you!"

Sara's little sister appeared at the door.
"Dinnertime!" she said.
"Thank goodness," Sara sighed.

At the dinner table, everyone had some advice for Sara.

"You know, Sara, maybe you are trying too hard," her father said.

"Or maybe, Sara, you are not trying hard enough," her grandmother added.

Soon everyone was talking all at once, waving their forks and spoons in the air.

"Do-it-like-this. . . ," said her father.

"Do-it-like-that. . . ," said her grandmother.

"Do-it-like-this-Sara-do-it-like-that. . . ," chanted her little sister, rocking in her chair.

In fact, everyone was so excited that almost no one noticed when Sara pushed her chair away from the table and, leaving her dessert, stomped out of the room.

Sara slammed the door to her room and sat down at her desk. Her paper was still a bright white. The paints in her paint box were still clean. Sara still hadn't painted the most wonderful painting that had ever been painted.

Sara sighed a little sigh and put her head on her desk.

When dinner was over, Sara's mother took a square of chocolate cake into Sara's room.

"Oh, Mommy," Sara said. "I was going to paint the earth and the sky and the day and the night, and the summer and the winter and the whole universe. But I can't."

"The universe is *very* big, Sara," her mother said.

Sara and her mother sat together by the window. The sky was just darkening. There was a bit of a bit of a moon.

"Remember, Sara," her mother said, "you can only begin at the beginning."

"But I don't even know where that is," Sara said.

They watched the windows of the houses across the street light up one by one.

"The universe is only people like you and me, and your desk and this room, and those houses . . ."

". . . and the tree outside my window?" Sara asked.

Her mother nodded.

They watched the leaves of the tree rustle in the evening wind.

Sara smiled. "I think I know where to begin now," she said.

Sara's mother gave her a kiss and left her to herself.

Sara pulled her chair up to her desk. She moved
her paper a little to the left and a little to the right.
She picked up the fat, round brush and dipped it
in the water in her jelly glass.

Sara swirled the brush in a tin of deep-brown
watercolor, and she began . . .